BOOK CLUB EDITION

WALT DISNEY'S
Peter Pan
AND CAPTAIN HOOK

from the motion picture based on the story by James M. Barrie

adaptation by
Mary Carey

Random House
New York

Adapted from the Walt Disney motion picture PETER PAN, by arrangement with The Hospital for Sick Children, London, England; Copyright 1911, 1921 by Charles Scribner's Sons; Copyright 1939 by Lady Cynthia Asquith, Peter L. Davies, and Barclay's Bank, Ltd.; published 1911 under the title, "Peter Pan and Wendy," and in 1950 under the title "Peter Pan."

Library of Congress Cataloging in Publication Data

Carey, Mary.   Peter Pan and Captain Hook.

Wendy tells her two brothers a bedtime story about Peter Pan's efforts to rescue Tiger Lily and Tinkerbell from Captain Hook. Based on Walt Disney's motion picture version of James Barrie's Peter Pan.

[1. Fantasy] I. Barrie, Sir James Matthew, bart., 1860-1937. Peter Pan. II. Peter Pan (Motion picture) III. Title PZ8.C189Pe [E] 72-4849 ISBN 0-394-82517-9   ISBN 0-394-92517-3 (lib. bdg.)

Manufactured in the United States of America

K

It was the best time of the day.
The lamps were lighted in the bedroom.
Wendy sat by the fire.

"Tell us a story, Wendy," said her brother
John. "A pirate story."

"With Indians in it!" cried Michael.

So Wendy told her brothers a story.
It had pirates and Indians in it.
But it began with Peter Pan.

Peter Pan was a boy.
He was very brave.
He could crow like a rooster.
Best of all he could fly.

He could fly high.

He could fly low.

He could race with the clouds. And chase the stars.

He could slide
down the rainbow.

Peter's best friend was
the tiny fairy Tinkerbell.
Tink could fly, too.

She never talked.
But she would stand
on Peter's hand.
Tiny lights flashed, and
she made tinkling sounds.

Peter could always understand her.

Peter and Tink lived in Neverland.
It was a magic place. Indians camped
in the woods. There was a pirate ship
in the bay near Skull Rock.
And there was Hangman's Tree.

Peter's home was a secret cave
under Hangman's Tree. He lived
in the cave with his friends.
These friends were the Lost Boys.
They had no mothers or fathers.
But they did have Peter and Tink
—and the safe, secret cave.

One day Peter and Tink went out flying.
The Lost Boys could not fly. They tried
to think of something else to do
—something that would be fun.

"I know!" said one. "Let's go
fight the Indians!"

"We can creep up on them,"
said another.

"We'll catch them!" cried a third.

They began creeping through the woods.
They were going toward the Indian camp.

"Shhh!" said one of the boys.
"An Indian may be hiding behind every tree."

There was not an Indian behind every tree.
There was an Indian *inside* every tree.

The Indians leaped out
and caught the Lost Boys.
"Help, Peter!" shouted the boys.
"Tinkerbell! Save us!"

Peter and Tinkerbell did not hear the boys.
Peter and Tink were on Skull Rock.

"Look!" said Peter. He pointed across the water.

Tink looked and saw a boat. In it she saw
Peter's enemy, the terrible pirate, Captain Hook.
She also saw Hook's mate, Mr. Smee.
And she saw Tiger Lily,
the beautiful Indian princess.

Tiger Lily was tied with thick ropes.
The poor girl was Captain Hook's prisoner.

Suddenly there was a loud *tick-tock, tick-tock*. It came from a crocodile swimming near the boat.

Captain Hook jumped out of the boat.
He climbed up onto the rock.

"That crocodile follows me everywhere!"
he cried. "He wants to eat me!"

"Lucky for you he swallowed that clock,"
said Smee. "The *tick-tock* always tells you
when he is near."

Smee lifted Tiger Lily onto Skull Rock.

"Tell me where Peter Pan lives," said Hook.
"Or you will never leave Skull Island!"

"You codfish!" shouted Peter, flying down.
He pulled Smee's cap over his eyes.

Then he flew over to Captain Hook
He pushed him right into the water.

Peter untied Tiger Lily. He carried her
up, up and away from Skull Rock.

Peter flew with Tiger Lily
to the Indian camp.
The Lost Boys were there.
They were still tied up.

Tiger Lily's father was at the camp, too.
He was a great chief, with many feathers
in his headdress.

"You saved Tiger Lily!" he said.
"Because of that we will let
your friends go. We will have
a feast, and sing and dance."

But . . .
where was Tinkerbell?

Tink had stayed at Skull Rock.
She was watching Captain Hook swim
away from the tick-tocking crocodile.

The Captain leaped from the water.
He was shaking with fear.
Tinkerbell laughed and laughed.

Suddenly, Mr. Smee popped his cap
over Tink. She stopped laughing.

"Cheer up, Captain," said Smee. "We have
lost Tiger Lily. But we have someone better.
We have Peter Pan's best friend, Tinkerbell!"

Peter Pan and the Lost Boys were leaving
the Indian camp.

It was very late. The deep forest was dark.
They needed Tinkerbell's flashing lights
to show them the way.

"Tink must be at home," said Peter.

They came to Hangman's Tree.
They stepped on a mushroom beside the path.
Then they pressed a knothole near a low branch.
The door to the secret cave opened.

No jingling, ringing sound greeted them.
No fairy light flashed out to cheer them.
The cave was empty.

"What has happened to Tinkerbell?"
cried Peter Pan.

Michael pulled at Wendy's hand.

"What did happen to Tinkerbell?" he asked.

"What did Captain Hook do with her?"

"He took her to the pirate ship," said Wendy.

"What then?" asked John.

Captain Hook and Mr. Smee plotted
a terrible plot. They wanted to make
Peter Pan come to the pirate ship to save
Tinkerbell. Then they would capture Peter.

The pirates locked Tinkerbell in a lantern
outside the ship's cabin. There she stayed,
tinkling—and shining—and calling for help.

But now Peter Pan was looking for Tinkerbell.
He flew here and there across Neverland.
Finally he saw the fairy light on the pirate ship.

Quickly Peter flew to Hangman's Tree.
"Captain Hook has Tinkerbell!"
he told the Lost Boys.
"We have to save her!"

Quietly, quietly, the boys swam
from the shore to the pirate ship.
Quietly, quietly, they climbed
up the rope and onto the deck.

Peter Pan flew to the top of the mast.
"Hook, you're a codfish!" he crowed.
The pirates rushed out onto the deck.

"It's Pan!" shouted Hook. "Fire the cannon,
Mr. Smee!"

Smee tried to fire the cannon.
But one of the boys ran off with his cannon ball.

Another boy chased Smee around the deck
with a shiny sword.

Peter Pan flew down from the mast.
He cut the feather off Captain Hook's hat.

The frightened pirate fell into the sea.
But who was waiting in the water?

The tick-tocking crocodile was waiting!
Captain Hook swam for his life.

He swam and he swam and he swam.
For all we know, he is swimming still.

Peter Pan and the Lost Boys let Tinkerbell
out of the lantern. Then they hurried
to their secret cave under Hangman's Tree.

"What happened then?" asked Michael.

"Peter Pan and Tinkerbell and the Lost Boys went to sleep," said Wendy. "And that's where you are going."

She tucked her brothers into bed.
"Is there really a Peter Pan?"
asked John. "Will we ever *see* him?"
"Perhaps some day," said Wendy.

Later that night a soft tinkling sound woke Wendy.
She saw a flickering light. Then a boy's shadow
flew past the window.

Wendy smiled. She had finally seen Peter Pan.
At least she had seen his shadow!
And she had heard Tinkerbell's tinkling sound.
Wendy's eyes closed again, and she was fast asleep.